This Little Tiger book belongs to:

_____

_____

_____

FOR JOHN, ALEX, JULIANNA AND MAX

-ALWAYS!
TS

TO AVA (ALL THE WAY TO THE MOON)

...AND TO KATY.
AG

LITTLE TIGER PRESS
1 The Coda Centre, 189 Munster Road,
London SW6 6AW
www.littletiger.co.uk
First published in Great Britain 2014
This edition published 2015

Text copyright © Tammi Salzano 2014
Illustrations copyright © Ada Grey 2014
Tammi Salzano and Ada Grey have asserted their
rights to be identified as the author and illustrator of this
work under the Copyright, Designs and Patents Act, 1988
A CIP catalogue record for this book is available
from the British Library
All rights reserved • ISBN 978-1-84895-875-3
Printed in China • LTP/1400/0926/0614
1 2 3 4 5 6 7 8 9 10

I Love You Just the Way You Are

TAMMI SALZANO

ADA GREY

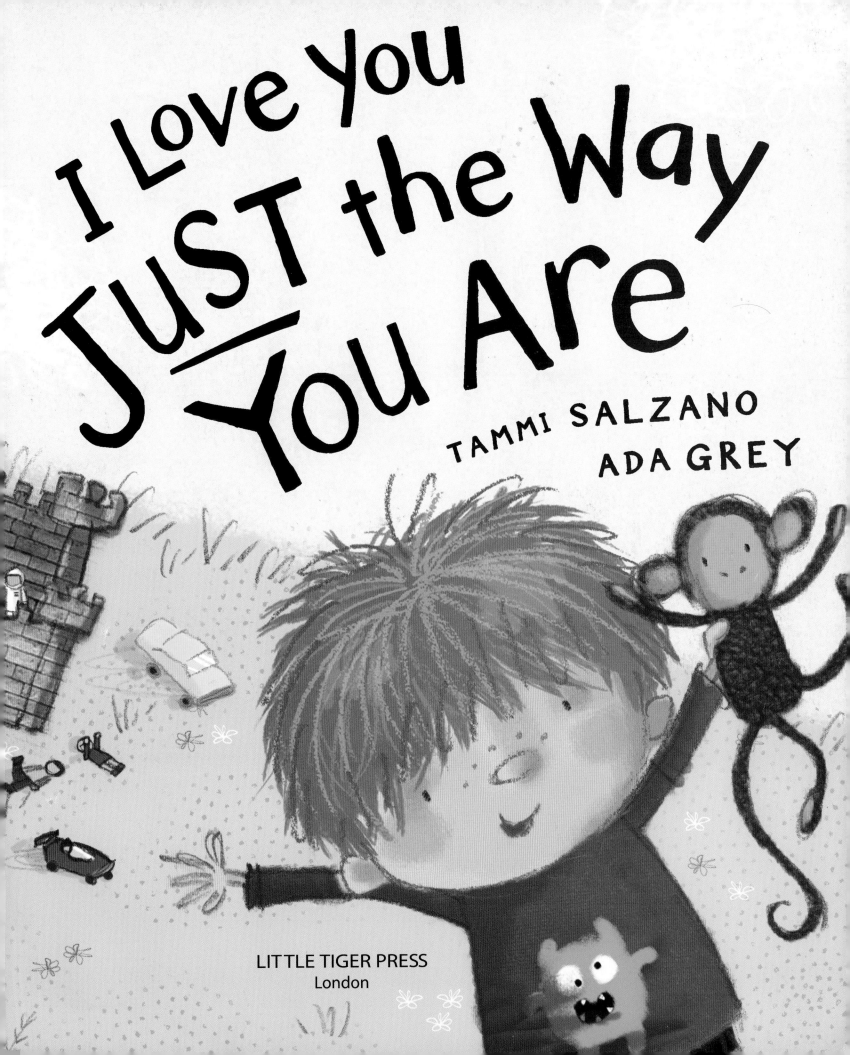

LITTLE TIGER PRESS
London

I love you in the morning
when the sun shines
on the day,

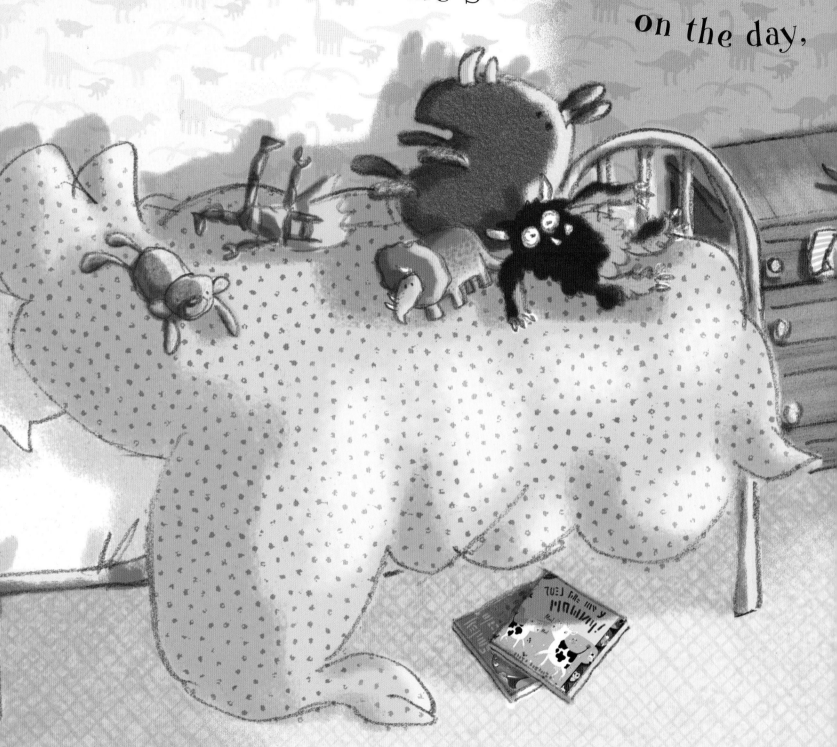

With silly hair that's sticking up each and every way.

I love you when you're playing –

blowing bubbles

in the sun,

Climbing **high**

and **sliding** down, having **so** much **fun!**

I love you when you're messy – sticky fingers, face and hair,

With papers scattered all around and paint splashed everywhere!

I love you when

we're quiet, sharing books and puzzles, too.

I treasure **every** moment of this
special time with
you.

I love you when you dress up

and pretend to be a king,

Or a superhero-pirate-dog

who loves to
dance and sing.

I love you when it's bath time,

squeaky-clean and smelling sweet,
Giggling as I scrub your ears,
tummy, hands,
and feet.

I love you when it's bedtime and you bounce into your bed.

I hold you close
to say goodnight

and
kiss
you on the
head.

I **love** your smile, freckles, **all** the **funny** things you **say**.

I love you just the way YOU are, and more and more each day!

More Little Tiger books
to share with your loved ones!

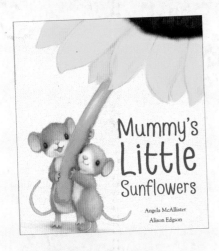

Mummy's
LITTLE
Sunflowers

Angela McAllister
Alison Edgson

My Dad!

Steve Smallman   Sean Julian

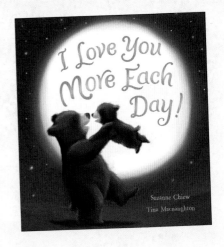

I Love You
More Each
Day!

Suzanne Chiew
Tina Macnaughton

I Love You
as
BIG
as the
World

David Van Buren   Tim Warnes

Big
and Small

Elizabeth Bennett
Jane Chapman

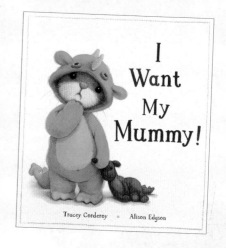

I
Want
My
Mummy!

Tracey Corderoy   Alison Edgson

For information regarding any of the above titles
or for our catalogue, please contact us:
Little Tiger Press, 1 The Coda Centre,
189 Munster Road, London SW6 6AW
Tel: 020 7385 6333 • Fax: 020 7385 7333
E-mail: contact@littletiger.co.uk
www.littletiger.co.uk